Carolina Friends School
Durham Early School

The Henderson Brothers,
Jonathan and David

I'll Always Love You

By HANS WILHELM

CROWN PUBLISHERS, INC. • NEW YORK

To Lea

Published by Crown Publishers, Inc., a Random House company,
225 Park Avenue South, New York, New York 10003.
CROWN is a trademark of Crown Publishers, Inc.
Manufactured in Belgium

Library of Congress Cataloging-in-Publication Data
Wilhelm, Hans
I'll always love you.
Summary: A child's sadness at the death of a beloved dog is tempered
by the remembrance of saying every night, "I'll always love you."
1. Children's stories, American. [1. Dogs—Fiction.   2. Death—
Fiction]   I. Title.   PZ7.W6481611   1985   [E]   84-20060
ISBN 0-517-55648-0
0-517-57265-6 (pbk.)
0-517-57759-3 (lib. bdg.)
10 9 8 7 6 5 4 3

This is a story about
Elfie — the best dog
in the whole world.

We grew up together, but Elfie grew
much faster than I did.

I loved resting my head on her warm
coat. Then we would dream together.

My brother and sister loved
Elfie very much, but she was
my dog.

Every day, Elfie and I
played together.

Elfie loved to chase squirrels

and to dig in my mother's flower garden.

Sometimes my folks would get very angry with Elfie when she would get into mischie. But they still loved her, even when they scolded her.

The trouble was, no one
told her except me.

The years passed quickly,
and while I was growing taller
and taller, Elfie was growing
rounder and rounder.

The older Elfie got,
the more she slept,
and the less
she liked to walk.
I was getting worried!

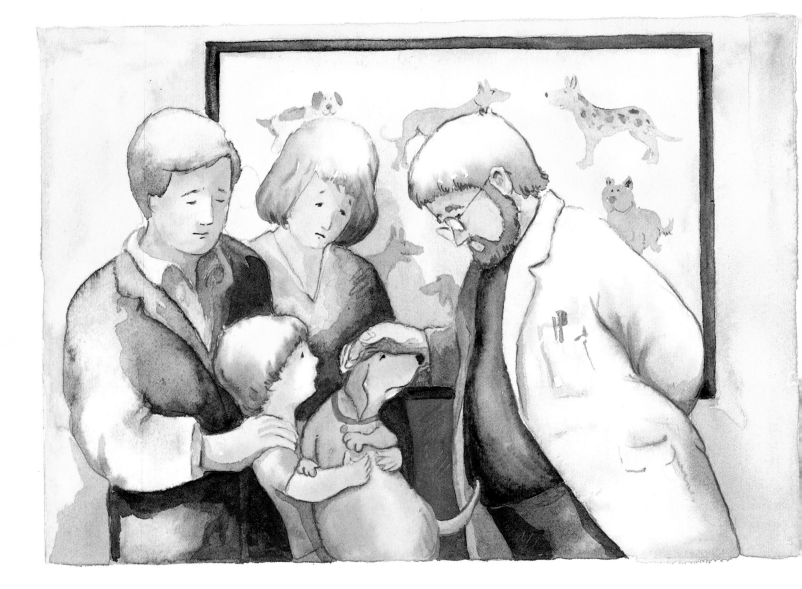

We took Elfie to the vet,
but there wasn't much he could do.
  "Elfie is just growing old,"
he said.

It soon became too difficult
for Elfie to climb the stairs.

But she *had* to sleep in my room.

I gave Elfie a soft pillow
to sleep on, and before
we went to sleep
I would say to her,
"I'll always love you."
I know she understood.

One morning I woke up
and discovered that Elfie
had died during the night.

We buried Elfie together.
We all cried and hugged
each other.

My brother and sister loved Elfie
a lot, but they never told her so.
　　I was very sad, too, but it helped
to remember that I had told her
every night, "I'll always love you."

A neighbor offered me a puppy.
I knew Elfie wouldn't
have minded, but I said no.

I gave him Elfie's basket instead.
He needed it more than I did.

Someday I'll have another dog,
or a kitten or a goldfish.
But whatever it is, I'll tell it
every night: "I'll always love you."